Monica
SELES

Monica SELES

RETURNING CHAMPION

Kristin Smith Fehr

Lerner Publications Company / Minneapolis

To my husband, Alan, for his support, my daughters, Karla and Laura, for their patience, and to the staff of the Dickinson Public Library, Dickinson, North Dakota, for their valuable assistance.

Information in this book came from the following sources: *Current Biography; Facts on File Yearbook; Forbes; Ladies of the Court: Grace and Disgrace on the Women's Tennis Tour,* by Michael Mewshaw; *Monica Seles Stat Page,* a web site maintained by Ed Zafian; *The New York Times; People Weekly; Publishers Weekly; The Sporting News; Sports Illustrated; Tennis; Time;* The Women's Tennis Association web site; *Vogue;* and *The Wall Street Journal.*

This book is available in two editions:
Library binding by Lerner Publications Company
Soft cover by First Avenue Editions
241 First Avenue North, Minneapolis, Minnesota 55401

LIBRARY OF CONGRESS CATALOGING-IN-PUBLICATION DATA

Fehr, Kristin Smith, 1960–
    Monica Seles : returning champion / Kristin Smith Fehr.
      p.   cm.
    Includes bibliographical references (p.) and index.
    Summary: A biography of the Yugoslavian tennis star, who won a Grand Slam title in 1989, and whose career was interrupted by a traumatic attack in which she was stabbed at a match in Germany in 1993.
    ISBN 0-8225-2899-1 (hc : alk. paper). — ISBN 0-8225-9773-X (pbk. : alk. paper)
    1. Seles, Monica, 1973–   —Juvenile literature. 2. Tennis players—Yugoslavia—Biography—Juvenile literature. 3. Women tennis players—Yugoslavia—Biography—Juvenile literature. [1. Seles, Monica, 1973– . 2. Tennis players. 3. Women—Biography.]
    I. Title.
GV994.S45F45   1997
796.342'092
[B]—dc21   96–52241

Manufactured in the United States of America
1 2 3 4 5 6 – JR – 02 01 00 99 98 97

Contents

Monica walks off the court between the first and second
sets of her exhibition match against Martina Navratilova.

1

Blocking Out the Fear

Monica Seles's racket connected squarely with the tennis ball, as if she were batting away the nightmares of the past 27 months. She raced around the court, lacing returns at her opponent's feet, tearing **forehands crosscourt,** and burying **backhands** in the corners.

It was July 1995, and Monica's main goal at the Return of the Champions event was to master her stage fright. The glaring lights of television cameras, noise coming from the casinos, a rustling crowd, and abrupt shouts all were unsettling. But they provided a good test for the young woman facing tennis legend Martina Navratilova. Gone from the tennis world since a crazed tennis fan stabbed her, Monica was playing in front of fans for the first time since the attack.

The day before, Monica and her parents arrived by private jet in Atlantic City, New Jersey, and took a limousine to Caesars. After stepping out of the car and onto a red carpet, Monica walked straight into a wall of photographers and sports reporters.

Monica was surrounded by a ring of security guards who helped her work her way inside the front door. An actress dressed like Cleopatra tossed a handful of rose petals at her in greeting, and Monica winced and turned away with a small squeal. It was the only time she really looked uncomfortable.

When she was stabbed, Monica was just 19 years old, with a full career ahead of her. She was ranked the number 1 women's tennis player in the world, and her life revolved around the game. But after physically recovering from the stab wound to her back, Monica became fearful that the man, Günther Parche, would come after her again. And because he stabbed her during a tennis match in Germany, in front of about 10,000 spectators, Monica felt she wouldn't even be safe on a tennis court.

In Atlantic City, much to her fans' relief, they saw the same player as two years before stroll confidently onto the court with Martina. As the applause steadily mounted and approached a din, the two chatted "about how nervous we were," Martina said.

Monica endured the noise until it reached a climax. Then she covered her face with her hands before regaining her composure. Monica curtsied to each grandstand. Then she and Martina high-fived.

After Monica won her match against Martina Navratilova, she joined her parents at courtside.

The match was a promising return to competitive tennis for Monica. She played the exhibition like the champion she was. After defeating Martina 6–3, 6–2, Monica rejoiced.

"This whole thing has been, like, one big wow," she told reporters. "I couldn't have asked more of myself."

And Martina, who helped Monica return to the game they both loved, rejoiced along with her friend. "Those **passing shots** were not a mirage," Martina told reporters. "She is here."

2

Lessons from Tom and Jerry

A tennis ball decorated with Tom and Jerry, the cat and mouse cartoon characters, zoomed through the air. Young Monica Seles studied it and pounced, stroking a perfect return.

To teach Monica the fundamentals of the game, her father, Karolj, used his skills as a cartoonist and film-maker to give lessons about the sport. By drawing cartoon characters on tennis balls, Karolj helped her to develop a killer's instinct. He told her she must go after her opponent as a cat goes after a mouse.

"My father's animated cartoons really helped me learn the right service motion," Seles recalled later. "Because he used cartoons and lots of humor, I always enjoyed practicing."

Monica began tennis lessons under Karolj Seles's watchful eye when she was just six years old. At first Monica was frustrated by her slow progress. She quit after a few months. A short time later, Monica's older brother, Zoltan (called the Z-man), brought home the winner's trophy from the Yugoslav Junior Tennis Championships. Seeing the trophy spurred Monica to resume tennis lessons.

With a bachelor's degree in physical education and tennis knowledge gleaned from books, Karolj taught the left-handed Monica an unusual two-handed swing for both her backhand and forehand. It became Monica's greatest weapon.

Monica and Zoltan (shown after Monica turned pro) both were talented tennis players growing up in Yugoslavia.

She was born to Karolj, a political cartoonist and documentary filmmaker, and Esther, a computer programmer, on December 2, 1973. Zoltan was eight. The Seleses lived in the Hungarian section of Serbia, a republic of the former Yugoslavia.

By the time she was eight years old, Monica was practicing tennis regularly with Zoltan and Karolj in a parking lot near their apartment. For a net, they would tie a string to the bumpers of two cars. Because of this, Yugoslavs would later call Monica "champion from the parking lots."

Aside from the amount of time she spent practicing tennis, Monica's childhood was typical. She remembers applying her mother's lipstick and dressing up in high heels, black lace, and lots of hats. She loved to dance and eagerly tried out for every play at her school. But the one she remembers most is the play in which she didn't get the part she wanted—because she couldn't do a handstand.

"I practiced for weeks, but I couldn't learn to do it because I had this little fear of heights," Monica said much later. "That failure stayed in my memory and it still makes me mad."

Monica took out some of that anger on the tennis court. With her father coaching her, Monica rapidly developed into an outstanding junior tennis player. In 1982, she won an important European tournament for players who were 12 years old and under. At the time, she couldn't keep score and didn't know when the match was over.

Monica traveled to the United States to compete against other young tennis hopefuls. Although she enjoyed American culture, she felt guilty about coming home with stuffed animals from Disney World when her friends didn't have anything like them.

"I didn't want them to think I was showing off. So I put them quietly away," Monica said. "I was aware of the differences, and I still am. No matter what happens, I don't want to forget where I came from or behave differently with my friends."

Growing up, Monica enjoyed going to basketball games with her father. Monica still remembers when a basketball star in Yugoslavia snubbed her request for an autograph. As she became more famous, she was determined to shake hands and give autographs to any youngsters who asked. "Maybe it'll make their day," she said. "It's part of the sport. A lot of kids look up to athletes."

Monica quickly tallied an impressive number of tennis wins, including consecutive victories at the European Championships. At 9 years old, Monica was her country's 12-and-under champion. By age 10, she was the European junior champion. When she was 12, she captured the 14-and-under division title at the European tournament and became the youngest girl ever to be named Yugoslavia's Sportswoman of the Year.

Before long, young Monica was impressing tennis experts worldwide with her incredible talent.

That same year, while watching a tournament in Florida, legendary tennis coach and trainer Nick Bollettieri saw Monica defeat one of his star pupils.

"I was so impressed that I offered Monica a full scholarship and invited the entire family to come and live at the academy," Bollettieri said later. "She was all feet and could barely see over the net, but could she play!"

Much different from other young tennis stars, Monica could practice for hours at a time and never lose her concentration, get upset, or utter a negative word.

While Monica polished her tennis game into one of the finest on the tennis tour, she also worked at projecting a glamorous image off the court.

3

The Spotlight

In 1986, Monica and her family moved to Bradenton, Florida, so 12-year-old Monica could attend Nick Bollettieri's tennis academy. Leaving Yugoslavia was hard for the close-knit family, but Karolj and Esther took two-year leaves of absence from their jobs so Monica could practice six hours a day with the famous coach.

In Yugoslavia most children leave their parents only when they marry, enter the army, or find the rare job that takes them to another city. Houses are passed down through generations.

But the Seleses' dreams took them far from the rest of their family. For Monica to be successful, she needed what Bollettieri could offer. Yugoslavia didn't have enough resources to help Monica develop into a premier player. Indoor courts were a 90-minute drive away, and **grass** and **hard courts** were few. Karolj wanted financial help and additional coaching for his daughter. He believed tennis was a way to a better life for his children. He was willing to uproot the family for a dream.

"Such sacrifice? I know, but that's the way it is," he told a reporter through an interpreter.

A few months after Monica arrived at Bollettieri's academy, she practiced with Jim Courier. Courier was destined to be one of the top players on the men's circuit, but he had trouble handling Monica's game on this day. With the first ball, Monica smacked a winner.

Moving to the warm climate of Florida in the United States gave Monica more opportunities to practice, especially on different types of court surfaces.

She did it again, impressing Courier with her ability to play and return balls. But after a few more balls were returned the same way over the next 15 minutes, Courier walked off the court in frustration, vowing never again to hit with Monica.

While at the tennis academy, Monica honed her game through practice sessions rather than in tournaments. She took a long break from playing any tournaments or matches. She worked to develop the power, finesse, and foot speed that she needed to be number 1 in women's tennis.

Nick Bollettieri (right, with Monica) ran a tennis academy that allowed young players—including Andre Agassi and Jim Courier—to hone their skills.

Monica made few tournament appearances during her first two years in the United States.

"Taking the pressure off helped me develop more. I could work on all kinds of new things and never worry about winning or losing," she said later. "I just love to play and practice. I love to learn new things. I got excited about getting better and making changes in my game."

Sidestepping tournaments avoided the huge amount of pressure that can be placed on rising tennis stars, but Monica was already famous. At times, Monica remembered, up to 100 kids were asking for autographs at her 9 A.M. practice sessions. "I always had to look my best on the court and I couldn't miss a volley. It was very hard on me mentally to do that every day," she recalled. So she closed her practice sessions.

At times Nick Bollettieri had trouble finding practice partners for Monica. The girls at Bollettieri's tennis academy refused to play against her because she hit the ball too hard, so the trainer arranged for boys to practice with Monica.

In 1987, Monica made her debut in a Virginia Slims tournament, and the next year she played in the Lipton International Players Championships. She competed as an amateur in both tournaments and lost in the early rounds.

But in 1989—her first season as a professional—Monica attracted the attention of the tennis world when she reached the semifinals of two tournaments, winning a match against the world's seventh-ranked player,

Manuela Maleeva-Fragniere, along the way. However, injuries forced her to forfeit both semifinal matches, and people worried that she was too small and frail to withstand the rigors of the professional tour.

Monica's breakthrough came in April 1989, in the final of a Virginia Slims tournament in Houston. Down a set to top-seeded tennis legend Chris Evert, Monica rebounded. She took the match with scores of 3–6, 6–1, and 6–4—earning her first professional championship. She was 15 years old, playing in her sixth professional event. The win put her in 23rd place in the world rankings of women tennis players.

After the tournament, Evert forecast a promising future for Seles. "I don't see any reason why Monica won't be in the top 10 and then the top 5," Evert said.

Monica rushes to the net after winning a 1989 tournament.

At the French Open in 1989, Monica's blasts proved too much for her opponents and pushed the rising star deep into her first Grand Slam tournament.

Far from being just another good tennis player, Monica soon proved she had star potential and a flair for self-promotion. The highest achievement in professional tennis is winning the Grand Slam, which means winning all four major titles—the Australian Open, the French Open, Wimbledon, and the U.S. Open—in the same calendar year. These four tournaments are also called the Grand Slam events. At the 1989 French Open, Monica's first Grand Slam event, she tossed roses to the crowd. Then she gave a bouquet to her third-round opponent, Zina Garrison, who was seeded fourth in the tournament.

Monica had a quick exit from her first Wimbledon. She said she had been so excited to see Princess Diana in the stands that she couldn't concentrate on her game.

Garrison didn't like the flowery show, but Monica took the contest in straight sets to advance to the quarterfinals. Then she won again, earning a spot in the semifinals against Steffi Graf. Graf was the world's top-rated woman player, going for her sixth consecutive Grand Slam crown.

Although Monica won one set, she lost her first Grand Slam event to the more experienced Graf. A month later, Monica made her Wimbledon debut, but lost to Graf in the fourth round. Monica then took a two-month break from tennis, returning to Yugoslavia.

She rejoined the tour at the U.S. Open in September 1989. There she faced Chris Evert in the fourth round for a highly publicized rematch. Although the media hyped the match as "passing the torch" from one generation of tennis stars to another, Chris dismissed Monica with scores of 6–0, 6–2.

At the end of the year, though, Monica's impressive string of accomplishments included reaching the quarterfinals in 8 of the 10 tournaments she had entered. As a result, she climbed from 86th to 6th place in the world rankings during the year.

Monica meets the press at the U.S. Open in 1989. Answering questions from the media after each match is a requirement of the women's tour.

The highlight of Monica's 1990 season—her second on the pro tour—was the French Open.

4

Taller, More Fearsome

By the beginning of the 1990 season, Monica had grown six inches in just 16 months. The growth spurt—to 5 feet, 9 inches tall—was hard for the teenager to adjust to and made her appear awkward in her first few matches of the season.

"The net seemed a different height, and the racket seemed lighter, like I was playing Ping-Pong," she told a reporter.

In addition to her sudden growth spurt, Monica was dealing with other situations. She was nursing a nagging shoulder injury and worrying about medical problems her mother was having. Monica lost in the early rounds of several tournaments. This included her first career loss in a first round.

Monica also had frequent feuds with Nick Bollettieri. Several times, Monica complained that Bollettieri was spending too much time on another rising star,

Andre Agassi. Finally, in March 1990, after Monica won the Lipton International Players Championships, the entire Seles family left Bollettieri's academy and moved to a private tennis facility in Sarasota, Florida.

A few weeks later, Monica infuriated Bollettieri by telling the media that her father had been her only coach. Bollettieri angrily replied he'd spent thousands of hours coaching Monica and thousands of dollars supporting the family's lifestyle.

The Seleses bid Nick Bollettieri farewell soon after Monica won the Lipton International Tournament. Monica would say later that Bollettieri forced her to leave the academy.

By the time she won this trophy at the West German Open in May 1990, Monica had climbed to the number 3 spot in the WTA rankings.

Monica put the controversy behind her and played well enough to rise to third place in the world standings by May 1990. That same month, Monica beat Martina Navratilova for the first time, winning the Italian Open final with a score of 6–1, 6–1. Martina later compared the match to being run over by a truck.

And a few days later, Monica posted her first victory in four meetings over Steffi Graf by winning the West German Open with a straight-set victory—snapping Steffi's 66-match winning streak. To capture the title, Monica relied on her trademark game: powerful two-handed **ground strokes;** strong, well-placed **returns of serves;** and fine **footwork.**

After winning her previous five tournaments, Monica turned to the French Open, grunting and grimacing as she unleashed her two-handed rockets. Along the way, she beat Jennifer Capriati, who—at 14 years old—was the youngest player ever to advance to the semifinals of a Grand Slam event. Then Monica again locked up with Steffi Graf in the final.

In the first set, which went to a **tiebreaker,** Monica fought off four consecutive set points. It was the match's turning point. After winning the first set 7–6 (8–6), Monica captured the second set, 6–4, to become the French Open's youngest champion in 103 years. The win gave 16-year-old Monica her second consecutive victory over Steffi and her first Grand Slam title. She was the youngest player to win a Grand Slam singles title since Lottie Dod in 1887.

"I've only lost to Monica twice, so she's not a nightmare yet," said Graf after the French Open. "I hope she doesn't become one."

To help herself win, Monica worked up some extra motivation before every tournament: She promised herself something special if she won. Until the French Open, she settled for buying things like a giant teddy bear or a leather jacket. But in Paris, she promised herself a bright yellow Lamborghini—an expensive sports car. "If I really want something, and I work hard, I'll get it," she told reporters with her unique giggle.

None of Monica's previous victories compared to winning her first Grand Slam—the French Open in 1990.

But although Monica won the tournament, her parents said no to the $130,000-plus car because they thought it was too expensive for someone so young.

Later in 1990, Monica played at Wimbledon, where her 36-match winning streak ended when she lost to Zina Garrison in the quarterfinals. The loss also ended Monica's six-tournament string of victories. Monica had an even earlier exit in the U.S. Open tournament, where she lost to the unseeded Linda Ferrando in the third round.

The losses disappointed Monica, and she became determined to improve her game on surfaces other than **clay courts.**

Jennifer Capriati, a fellow teen sensation on the tour, chats with Monica during a break in their tennis activities.

Monica kept a busy schedule of hard-court events during the fall of 1990. The highlight was the Virginia Slims Championships in New York City, a unique event that required the winner to take three sets in the final, rather than the usual two sets.

In the final, Monica faced Gabriela Sabatini, the 1990 U.S. Open winner, in five sets that lasted 3 hours and 47 minutes. After the lengthy battle, Monica emerged with her first Virginia Slims Championship and her 10th career title. The match score was 6–4, 5–7, 3–6, 6–4, 6–2. She was the tournament's youngest ever champion.

The match itself was a novelty too. For the first time in tour history, a women's match went to five sets. In every other tournament, matches were limited to three sets.

In 1990, Monica's tour earnings tallied more than $1.6 million. That money, combined with the $6 million she received from endorsement contracts and appearance fees, put her 12th among athletes in money earned. Monica quickly developed celebrity status and started appearing on the covers of magazines as a fashion model. She made far more money from modeling and for endorsing rackets, bottled water, cameras, tennis shoes, and hair care products than she made from playing in tennis tournaments.

Exhausted after beating Gabriela Sabatini in five sets, Monica struggles to hold the huge trophy.

The 1991 season started fantastically for Monica. She won the first Grand Slam event of the year—the Australian Open. She gained the tour's number 1 ranking in March by reaching the finals of a tournament in Palm Springs, California. Then she won the French Open for the second straight year.

Monica had a lot of reasons to clap in 1991.

Despite Monica's phenomenal success on the tennis court and her flair for publicity, her 1991 season was marred by controversy off the court.

In June, for example, top-seeded Monica withdrew without explanation from Wimbledon just three days before the prestigious tournament began. Eventually, Monica's agent told tennis officials that Monica had suffered injuries in a minor accident but gave no further details.

Since Monica hadn't given any proof of her injury, the Women's Tennis Association (WTA) fined her $6,000. Monica avoided the public spotlight during her absence, which added to media speculation about the real reasons she pulled out.

Her actions gave the impression that "pro tennis players are rich prima donnas who don't have respect for the work they must do," said Pam Shriver, a tour player who also served as president of the WTA Players Association. The controversy made Monica unpopular with other players.

"Any teen would have difficulty handling the role of No. 1 perfectly. And Seles has shown moments of immense maturity," Shriver wrote in an editorial in *Tennis* magazine. "Still, the top player must realize she has responsibilities: To play a solid schedule of tour events, to attend important sponsor functions and to offer an explanation when she does something as drastic as withdrawing from Wimbledon."

After weeks of hiding out, Monica resurfaced at an exhibition tournament in Mahwah, New Jersey. Holding her terrier, Astro, she explained at a packed press conference that severe leg pain, later diagnosed as shinsplints and a stress fracture, caused her to miss Wimbledon. But because she broke with the WTA's rules and resumed her playing schedule at a non-tour competition, the WTA fined Monica $20,000 more.

Later, before the finals of the Mahwah tournament, Monica announced she wouldn't play in the upcoming Federation Cup—a women's team competition organized by the International Tennis Federation. She refused to represent Yugoslavia, she said, because of the way the government had treated her and her family before they moved to Florida. She had often said how difficult it had been for her to pursue tennis in Yugoslavia. Not only did her family have to fight for adequate training facilities, they had to overcome a perception that trying to launch a top-level tennis career would be too hard on a girl.

Even though she had a doctor's note citing the same injury that kept her out of Wimbledon, the ITF punished Monica for backing out of the Federation Cup. They banned her from competing in the 1992 Summer Olympic Games.

By the time of the U.S. Open in September 1991, Monica had become so unpopular that fans repeatedly jeered at her during matches, particularly in the semifinals and in the finals. In the semis, Monica and her best friend on the tour, Jennifer Capriati, faced each other in a memorable, hard-hitting contest. Two points from defeat in the third set, Monica squeezed out a victory, 6–3, 3–6, 7–6 (7–3). A reporter for *Sports Illustrated* later called the pairing "the most extraordinary match ever between two players—male or female—under the age of 18."

At 17, Monica was the top player in women's tennis.

She had a new hairstyle, but Monica played her usual dominating game at the U.S. Open.

In the U.S. Open finals, Monica again met up with 34-year-old Martina Navratilova. Martina won the first set on a tiebreaker. But after that, Monica came on strong and claimed her third Grand Slam title of the year. During the 1991 season, she earned more than

$2.4 million from tournaments. She also had held the number 1 ranking for most of the year and sealed the top position with another win in the Virginia Slims Championships.

Monica started 1992 much as she had ended the previous season—by winning Grand Slam events. She beat Mary Jo Fernandez, 6–2, 6–3, in the final to claim the Australian Open. Her string of winning 27 matches and reaching 21 tournament finals ended at the Lipton International Players Championship, with a loss to Jennifer Capriati in the quarterfinals.

Then she met up with Steffi Graf in the finals of the French Open. In a grueling match that lasted 2 hours and 43 minutes, Monica came out ahead, 6–2, 3–6, 10–8. It was her third straight title at Roland Garros, the site of the French Open.

Monica had won both of the Grand Slam events thus far in 1992, and reporters began to wonder if she could win the third, at Wimbledon. It was the one major tournament she had yet to win—or even in which she had yet to advance to the finals. Tennis experts seemed to agree that Monica would never get past Graf for the title. Steffi already had three titles at Wimbledon, and her game was well-suited to the grass courts at the All England Club.

Monica geared up for the challenge of playing on grass and trying to beat Graf, but she wasn't ready for the peculiar distractions of Wimbledon. Monica was known for letting out loud grunts with her powerful strokes. Over the years, she had been teased for the sound effects. At Wimbledon the ridiculing became worse when a reporter brought a device that supposedly could measure the loudness of Monica's grunts. He called it a "Gruntometer" and said Monica's grunts were as loud as a freight train.

Monica might have been able to ignore the insults and focus only on tennis, but the attention prompted her opponents to complain to the umpires about the noises. A few times, officials warned Monica to quiet down. Even so, Monica advanced to the finals for the much-anticipated match against Steffi. There, she succeeded in holding in her grunts. She also lost the match, 6–2, 6–1.

With her quest for a Grand Slam in 1992 ended, Monica traveled from Wimbledon to two smaller tournaments and lost both times, still trying to play quietly. By the time Monica rolled into New York for the U.S. Open, she had put the whole, humiliating Wimbledon experience behind her. In fact, Monica won the tournament—noisily—without losing a single set. The only other players to have done that at the U.S. Open were Chris Evert and Martina Navratilova.

Monica won the last tournament of the year, the Virginia Slims Championships, for the third straight time. She held the number 1 ranking all year and finished the season with $2.6 million in prize money.

An umpire cautions Monica about making noises during matches. Monica's tennis suffered when she stayed quiet.

As great as her season had been, Monica hinted the best was yet to come. "I still have a lot to learn," she told reporters. She said she wanted to improve her **volleying**—her ability to rush the net. "I do it quite well in practice," she said. "But under pressure [in tournaments], I stick to my basics."

The big question for 1993 was whether Monica could finally win at Wimbledon and complete the Grand Slam. Most tennis experts predicted Monica would again dominate the field and retain the number 1 ranking. She quickly set about proving them right with yet another win at the Australian Open, her third in as many years. The future did indeed look bright for Monica.

Monica's string of successes on the court came to a halt because of a deranged tennis fan.

5

Darkness

Monica showed a flamboyant side of her personality from her earliest days in pro tennis. She constantly changed her hairstyles and hair colors, held many press conferences, and disappeared from the public eye—only to reappear later in some dramatic way.

By 1993, 19-year-old Monica often worried about the dangers of fame, despite her love of publicity. To keep herself safe, she wore disguises in public and made extra airplane reservations when traveling. She had been receiving death threats—including a bomb scare at the previous year's Wimbledon.

Since 1991, Monica's homeland had been embroiled in war. Fierce fighting broke out between different ethnic groups in Yugoslavia, especially between Serbs and Croats. Although she is an ethnic Hungarian, Monica is one of the world's most famous Serbs. Because of that, Monica received threats from Croats.

She became fearful and somewhat withdrawn from the public. "My life is a prison," she once said. "It gets pretty scary sometimes."

Monica's fears came true on April 30, 1993, while she was competing in the quarterfinals of the Citizens Cup tournament in Hamburg, Germany. During a break in her match against Magdalena Maleeva of Bulgaria, Monica sat in a chair alongside the court. Just then a man reached out from the stands behind her and stabbed her with a nine-inch, curved, serrated boning knife!

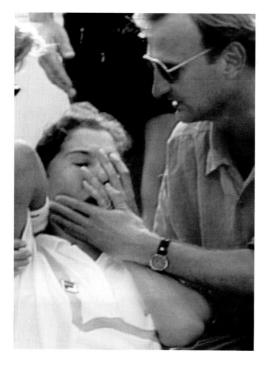

A shocked Monica gets help from a spectator seconds after the attack.

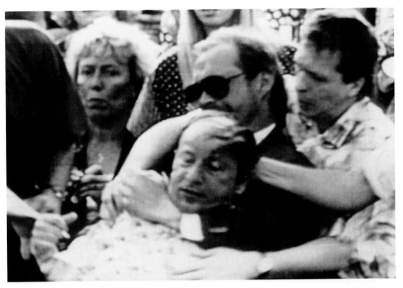

A security officer and several bystanders quickly subdued Günther Parche after he stabbed Monica.

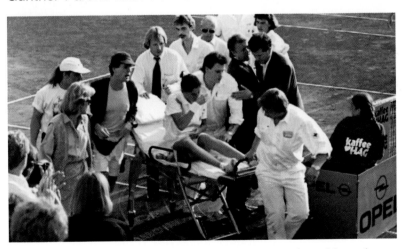

With Zoltan (in blue cap and maroon sweater) rushing along-side the gurney, paramedics wheel Monica off the court.

Oddly enough, the attack had nothing to do with the situation in Yugoslavia. The man was quickly subdued and was later found to be an unemployed German. Günther Parche told police he wanted to hurt Monica so his favorite player and Monica's chief rival, Steffi Graf, could regain the number 1 ranking.

Several months after the attack, Parche left jail. He was found guilty of stabbing Monica but didn't serve any further jail time. He would have to check in with probation officials regularly over the next two years.

Monica suffered a slightly torn muscle in the attack and had a deep puncture wound very close to her spinal cord. Doctors said she might have been paralyzed if the spinal cord had been cut. Monica recuperated in a German hospital for three days, then flew to the United States for tests. All the while, Steffi Graf was stunned that someone calling himself a fan of hers would hurt another player. She visited Monica in the hospital, and the two players cried together over the tragedy.

Monica's physical wounds healed quickly. After basic rehabilitation at a clinic in Vail, Colorado, she was soon working out and pretending the stabbing never happened. Monica worked harder than ever, training with track-and-field coach Bobby Kersee and Olympic gold medalist Jackie Joyner-Kersee. Rumors of a comeback spread, and Monica talked of returning to the tour in time for the Australian Open in January 1994. She felt good and had even held up during her father's operation for stomach cancer in December.

But then came Christmas 1993 and her first break since beginning rehabilitation. Until then she had been concentrating so much on recovering her game that she hadn't allowed herself to think about the stabbing. When she finally took a break, the emotions caught up with her. "Darkness was everywhere," she said later. Suddenly, she feared going to sleep in her Sarasota, Florida, home because the man might find her there. And she was haunted by replays of her own voice, howling as she was stabbed.

"My scream is what stayed with me a long time," she said. "I pretty much moved to daylight sleeping times. I couldn't sleep at night. I saw shadows in every corner.

"I would be up all night in my room, just sitting. In the dark or light, I didn't feel comfortable leaving the house. Total depression. I was just reliving that moment."

Monica's moods went up and down. In February, Zoltan and Karolj insisted Monica get help, so she began seeing a sports psychologist, Jerry Russel May, in Nevada. Sometimes she talked every day by telephone to May. She spoke to other victims of similar crimes. She was sure that, somehow, the stabbing had been her fault. "Why was it me?" Monica asked. "It changed my daily life."

It took Monica seven more months to begin piecing together a life outside of tennis. She became a United States citizen after living in the United States for eight years. At the May 1994 ceremony in Miami, Florida, the Yugoslavian-born athlete called it "a happy day for me. I am proud to be a United States citizen and look forward to continuing our lives here." Then Monica developed hobbies. She learned to operate a Jet Ski, took up waterskiing, read several books, and took French, guitar, and pool lessons.

The long delay in Monica's return to the tour made people wonder if she had played her last Grand Slam event in 1993 at the Australian Open.

During the time she stayed away from the tennis world, Monica grew an inch and gained some weight. She also weathered controversies from both the Women's Tennis Association and from Fila, one of her sponsors.

Just days after the stabbing, the women tennis pros voted to protect Monica's number 1 ranking until she recovered. When her wounds healed, but she didn't return to the tour, the ranking was dropped.

After having her life shattered by the stabbing, Monica had to work at regaining her love of life.

Monica's delay in coming back also caused Fila to sue her for breaking her contract with them. The Italian manufacturer of sneakers and sports clothing had signed Monica to promote its products when she was just 15 years old. The company said Monica promised to return to the tour three different times, but she didn't. In the meantime, Fila had turned out a Monica Seles line of tennis clothes and estimated more than $3 million in lost sales because Monica didn't resume playing.

Monica's other sponsors—who altogether would have paid her about $6 million—simply didn't pay Monica during her absence. Some said they kept a "harmonious relationship" and even coordinated new product development with her.

Monica denied Fila's accusations and a rumor that she stayed away from the tour to collect a big insurance check. She insisted that she wasn't faking the anguish that kept her from resuming her tennis career.

"I love to play tennis, and for the past 2½ years, I have lost all my income," Monica told a reporter for *Sports Illustrated*. "I've not received anything from the endorsements, and I've never had an insurance policy. Why wouldn't I play? It doesn't make any sense."

Monica greets many of her fans during her first tournament back on the women's tour.

6

Back in the Groove

For more than two years, Monica had stayed away from the spotlight, training on one of her home's two tennis courts. In her time away from tennis, Monica grew to 5 feet, 10½ inches. She was 21 years old. Emotionally and physically, she had grown up.

While Monica's friends and fans awaited her return, Monica came to realize that just hitting the tennis ball with Karolj or Zoltan wasn't enough. She needed to play competitively again. She contacted her former coach, Nick Bollettieri, and asked him to send over some hitting partners. She tired them out, Bollettieri said.

Eventually, Monica knew she was ready for a comeback. Martina Navratilova had retired from tennis in 1994, but was still active behind the scenes. She urged Monica to return to the tour and proposed an exhibition match between them to ease the way. The match would be meaningless, but it would give Monica a chance to play in front of her fans again.

Monica's first public match since the stabbing gave her fans—and tour officials—a lot of hope. Arriving in Atlantic City on July 28, 1995, Monica told reporters she couldn't be happy without tennis.

"You're here on this earth to be happy," Monica said before the match. "I'll never forget what happened. I'm just going to play great tennis and have fun."

In her match against Martina, Monica showed a lot of confidence. Her nervousness disappeared the first time she connected squarely with the ball, and she defeated Martina 6–3, 6–2. Sportswriters called the exhibition a healing experience for Monica. They said Monica was the same player as always, just a little taller and heavier.

Monica had made a high number of **unforced errors** and her rusty serve resulted in six **double faults.** Even so, Martina predicted Monica would need little time to readjust to the WTA tour.

Plans were made for Monica's return. At Martina's urging, the WTA had agreed to co-rank Monica number 1 with Steffi Graf for Monica's first six events or for 12 months, whichever came first.

A new deal with Nike was part of Monica's comeback. In July 1995, she ended her association with Fila and signed a multimillion-dollar, long-term agreement with Nike to endorse clothing and shoes.

Martina Navratilova wishes Monica well after they played the match that launched Monica's comeback.

During her long absence from the tennis circuit, Monica gained weight, but she told reporters she had no plans to diet. She said preoccupation with weight is a losing game.

"I gained some weight in the time I was off because my body was so used to working hard, and it didn't work hard," Monica said. "And I was under pressure and I ate maybe more than I should have." Tennis media guides listed Monica at 145 pounds, but she said she doesn't worry about her weight. "It is not a priority for me. As long as I'm able to move and I feel good, it doesn't matter."

A few weeks after playing Martina, Monica claimed the Canadian Open championship title. A typical women's tennis match lasts 1½ hours. Monica first defeated Kimberly Po in 60 minutes. Then 17 hours later, she beat Nathalie Tauziat in just 56 minutes. Two rounds later, in the finals, Monica ousted Amanda Coetzer, 6–0, 6–1, in another quick match to win the title.

Gabriela Sabatini embraces Monica after their semifinal match in the Canadian Open.

With a wave, Monica acknowledges cheering fans at the awards ceremony following her finals loss to Steffi Graf (left).

Obviously warmed up and back in stellar form, Monica went to New York and played her way to the U.S. Open finals, where she faced Steffi Graf. It was the biggest test of her comeback. Monica's lethal two-handed backhand kept the match lively—and the fans guessing—until the fourth game of the third set. That's when Steffi, who said she felt "absolute relief" in meeting Monica in the finals, dumped a low fore-hand shot. Although Steffi won, 7–6, 0–6, 6–4, Monica rushed the net to hug and kiss her.

"It's even more important [than winning] to see her play that well and obviously enjoy herself and be so at peace with herself. It's so great to see that," Steffi said later.

For her win in Toronto at the Canadian Open and for reaching the finals of the U.S. Open, the WTA named Monica the Comeback Player of the Year. However, her successful return came with a price: loss of privacy. Now when Monica goes out, she wears baggy clothes, thick glasses, and lets down her hair.

Monica's next big match was the Australian Open in January 1996. She overcame an injured shoulder and a pulled groin muscle to beat Anke Huber, 6–4, 6–1, in the final, winning her first Grand Slam event in three years. Monica's victory marked an important milestone in her recovery from the stabbing, which happened just a few months after she won her third Australian Open. The title was her ninth Grand Slam win, and it reaffirmed her status as co-number 1 with Steffi Graf—even though Steffi had missed the tournament while recovering from foot surgery.

Monica said winning the Australian Open was very emotional for her. "I cannot believe, still, that I'm here," Monica told the crowd as she smiled and tried to hold back tears. Her father, Karolj, wiped away his own tears as he listened to her. "I left this tournament in 1993 with unbelievable memories," Monica said. "The hardest thing for me, the time that I couldn't play, was not being able to defend my title here."

Monica had again proved herself a champion. She overcame the physical and mental scars and once more held above her head a Grand Slam trophy.

The trophy came at a cost, however. During the tournament, Monica experienced tendinitis (irritation and swelling) in her left shoulder. Then a medical test showed she had a small tear in the lining of her shoulder socket.

The injury forced Monica to withdraw from one tournament and then hampered her throughout the 1996 season. She still played well at times, winning five tournaments—including the Canadian Open for the second year in a row.

Monica had a fine 1996 season, but a shoulder injury slowed her efforts to regain sole possession of the number 1 spot. She came close, though.

Monica had mixed showings in the remaining major events. At the French Open, she played through the first four rounds before losing to Jana Novotna, 7–6 (9–7), 6–3, in the quarterfinals. She was quickly ousted from Wimbledon with a loss in the second round. In late July, Monica represented the United States in the Olympics, but again lost to Novotna in the quarterfinals.

At the U.S. Open, Monica regained her form. She cruised through the early rounds and met up with Steffi Graf once again in the finals. Graf had the better game, though, and won, 7–5, 6–4.

The season-ending Chase Championships rolled around in mid-November, but Monica's shoulder was so sore by then that she withdrew from the tournament. She still managed to climb back to the number 2 spot in the year-end rankings. Only Steffi Graf ranked higher. Perhaps it would only be a matter of time before Monica would again overtake her long-time rival in the standings and once more be the best women's player in tennis.

Career Highlights

Year	Year-End Ranking	Tournaments Played	Tournaments Won	Matches Won-Lost	Grand Slams Won
1988	86	3	0	5-3	0
1989	6	10	1	33-8	0
1990	2	15	9	54-6	1
1991	1	16	10	74-6	3
1992	1	15	10	70-5	3
1993	8*	4	2	17-2	1
1994	Did not compete				
1995	1**	2	1	11-1	0
1996	2	12	5	41-6	1
Totals	—	77	38	305-37	9

* *Monica's 1993 ranking includes only the four tournaments she played. At the time of the stabbing, she was ranked number 1.*

** *Monica was ranked number 1 with Steffi Graf through an agreement with the WTA.*

Major accomplishments:

- Australian Open Champion, 1991, 1992, 1993, 1996.
- French Open Champion, 1990, 1991, 1992.
- U.S. Open Champion, 1991, 1992.
- WTA Comeback Player of the Year, 1995.
- Associated Press Female Athlete of the Year, 1991.

Glossary

backhands: Ground strokes hit by reaching across the body. For a left-hander like Monica, this means hitting a ball that comes to the right side of her body.

clay courts: Playing surfaces made from clay or some claylike material. Balls hit on clay courts generally travel slower than balls hit on grass courts.

crosscourt: From one corner of the court to the corner diagonally across the net.

double faults: Situations in which neither of a player's serves for a point lands in her opponent's service box.

footwork: Positioning and using the feet to move into the right spot for returning the ball.

forehands: Ground strokes hit by extending the racket hand outward. For a left-hander like Monica, this means hitting a ball that comes to the left side of her body.

grass courts: A playing surface marked on closely cut grass. Balls hit on grass courts usually travel very fast.

ground strokes: Strokes used to hit the ball after it has bounced on a player's side of the court.

hard courts: Playing surfaces made from materials such as concrete, asphalt, or—very rarely—wood. Balls hit on these surfaces usually travel very fast.

passing shots: Strokes that drive the ball to one side of and past an opponent.

returns of serves: Hitting an opponent's serves back over the net. Monica is one of the best at placing her returns to make opponents scramble for the ball.

tiebreaker: A 12-point playoff to determine the winner of a set after both players have won six games. One player must win at least seven points and at least two more than the opponent. When a match's score is written down, any tiebreaker scores are shown in parentheses.

unforced errors: A point that a player loses because of her own mistake rather than because of a good shot by an opponent.

volleying: Hitting shots without letting the ball touch the ground.

ACKNOWLEDGMENTS

Photographs are reproduced by permission of: © Carol L. Newsom, pp. 1, 2, 10, 12, 15, 16, 18, 19, 20, 22, 24, 25, 28, 34, 37, 50, 59; Reuters/Gary Cameron/Archive Photos, pp. 6, 9, 55; Allsport/Simon Bruty, pp. 23, 26, 49; Reuters/Michael Urban/Archive Photos, p. 29; Reuters/Bettmann, pp. 31, 42, 45 (top), 46; Reuters/Dominic Wong/Archive Photos, p. 32; Reuters/Michael Cardwell/Archive Photos, p. 33; Allsport/Dan Smith, p. 38; Allsport, p. 41; Reuters/TV/Archive Photos, p. 44; Reuters/STR/Archive Photos, p. 45 (bottom); Allsport/Matthew Stockman, pp. 52, 56; and © John Klein, p. 57.

Front cover photographs are reproduced by permission of Archive Photos (large photo), and Rich Kane/SportsChrome East/West (small photos). Back cover photograph is reproduced by permission of © Carol Newsom.

Index